This Book Belongs To :

_____

_____

_____

Dedicated to my loving children,

Penelope & Byron.

To all the littlest adventurers, like Danielle, explore your world, feel your feelings, and never stop believing in your own strength!

Danielle loved her town by the water.

Her hair sparkled like sunshine
and her eyes danced with laughter.

But Danielle had a secret fear.

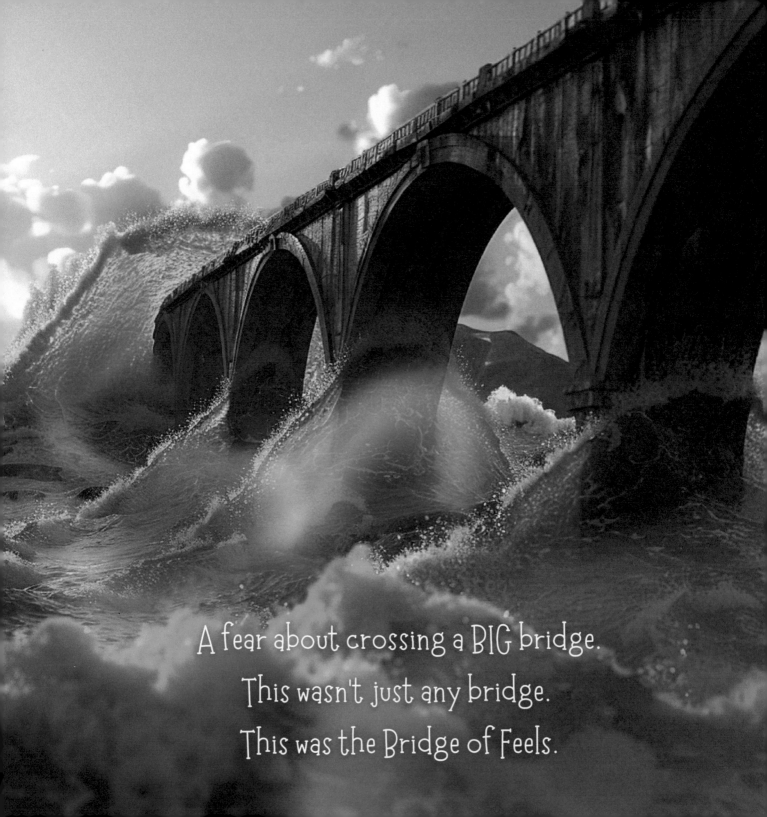

A fear about crossing a BIG bridge.

This wasn't just any bridge.

This was the Bridge of Feels.

The river below swirled with colorful emotions —
happy yellows, silly pinks, even angry reds.

But the scariest were the dark blue waves of
worries and deep purples of sadness.

When Danielle had to cross the Bridge of Feels her legs felt wobbly and her breath got stuck in her throat.

She decided in order to overcome her fear she had to keep crossing the bridge.

This time she didn't go alone.
She clung her sweaty grip onto
her Dad's hand extra tight.

Halfway across at the tippy top,
the bridge rumbled
and rain started to fall.

The river of emotions churned way down below.

A cold gust of wind swept through Danielle.

The other side of the bridge was no longer in sight.

Dad knelt down, his voice gentle.

"What feels are you having little one?"

"Scared ... and sad" Danielle sniffled.

Dad smiled. "It's okay to feel scared sometimes, everyone does!"

He said. "Big scared feelings can make it hard to take a step."

He pointed to the dark waves.
"See those? They're like your fears.
They're just water. They can't hurt you!"

Danielle took a deep breath.

She imagined her fear as a tiny shadow next to her.

"It's okay, little fear," she whispered.
"We can do this together."

A warm feeling spread through her,
all the way to her toes.

Slowly, she took a small step, then another.

The bridge creaked, the wind blew,

but Danielle kept going.

With each step, the scary waves seemed smaller, and the sadness faded. Finally, she reached the other side!

"You did it, Danielle!" Dad cheered.

"The Bridge of Feels is part of life, but you crossed it bravely, with kindness for yourself and all your feels."

Looking ahead, Danielle saw more bridges over sparkling rivers. She could face any bridge, any feeling, that life threw her way.

But now, she had a secret superpower – her own strength! And just then a tiny voice whispered in her heart.

"Remember, Danielle, you are...

braver than you believe!"

Meet Danielle Gould

Danielle loves writing stories just like this one!

Did you know she used to be scared of crossing a big bridge on her town too?

When Danielle was young (around your age!), her dad died. It made her feel sad and scared sometimes, just like Danielle in this book. But she discovered a special trick: whenever she felt those big emotions, she'd walk across the bridge.

With each step, she felt closer to her dad, even though he wasn't there anymore. ✨
Now, Danielle isn't scared of the bridge, in fact, she uses it to help her write stories about brave kids like you!

Do you have a special place that helps you feel close to someone you love?

Made in the USA
Columbia, SC
01 September 2024

41401456R00015